THE RUNAWAY TRAIN

For Miles Butcher

THE RUNAWAY TRAIN
A HUTCHINSON BOOK 978 1 862 30211 2 (from January 2007)
1 862 30211 1

First published in Great Britain by Julia MacRae,
an imprint of Random House Children's Books

Julia MacRae edition published 1995
Red Fox edition published 1997
This edition published 2006

3 5 7 9 10 8 6 4

Red Fox Books are published by Random House Children's Books,
61–63 Uxbridge Road, London W5 5SA,
a division of The Random House Group Ltd,
in Australia by Random House Australia (Pty) Ltd,
20 Alfred Street, Milsons Point, Sydney, NSW 2061, Australia,
in New Zealand by Random House New Zealand Ltd,
18 Poland Road, Glenfield, Auckland 10, New Zealand,
and in South Africa by Random House (Pty) Ltd,
Isle of Houghton, Corner Boundary Road & Carse O'Gowrie,
Houghton 2198, South Africa

THE RANDOM HOUSE GROUP Limited Reg. No. 954009
www.**kids**at**randomhouse**.co.uk

A CIP catalogue record for this book is available from the British Library.

Printed in China

THE RUNAWAY TRAIN

Benedict Blathwayt

RED FOX

Duffy Driver overslept.
Everyone was waiting at the
station for the little red train.

When Duffy was ready to start, he saw an old lady running down the platform. "I'll help you," he said. But he forgot to put the brake on and the little red train set off down the track . . . *Chuff-chuff, chuff-chuff, whoo . . . oooo*

Duffy saw a lorry. "Stop!" Duffy shouted. "I must catch up
with the runaway train!"
"Jump in," cried the lorry driver and off they went after the
little red train . . . *Chuff-chuff, chuff-chuff, whoo . . . oooo . . .*

. . . until they came to a traffic jam.

Duffy saw a boat. "Ahoy there!" Duffy shouted. "I must catch
up with the runaway train!"
"All aboard," cried the boatman and off they all went after the
little red train . . . *Chuff-chuff, chuff-chuff, whoo . . . oooo . . .*

. . . until the river turned away from the railway.

Duffy saw some bicycles. "Help!" Duffy shouted. "I must catch up with the runaway train!"
"Jump on," cried the cyclists and off they all went after the little red train . . . *Chuff-chuff, chuff-chuff, whoo . . . oooo . . .*

. . . until they ran into a flock of sheep.

Duffy saw some ponies. "Whoa!" Duffy shouted. "I must catch
up with the runaway train!"
"Up you come," cried the riders and off they all went after the
little red train . . . *Chuff-chuff, chuff-chuff, whoo . . . oooo . . .*

. . . until the ponies could go no further.

Duffy saw a tractor. "Halloo!" Duffy shouted. "I must catch up
with the runaway train!"
"Get on then," cried the farmer and off they went after the little
red train . . . *Chuff-chuff, chuff-chuff, whoo . . . oooo . . .*

. . . until they were spotted by a helicopter pilot.

"My last chance!" gasped Duffy. "I must catch up with the
runaway train!"
"Climb in quick," said the pilot and Duffy climbed in, while the
lorry driver, the boatman, the cyclists, the riders and the farmer
all stood and watched . . .

as Duffy caught up with the runaway train . . . *Chuff-chuff,*
chuffitty-chuff, whoo . . . oo . . . oo

And Duffy Driver drove the little red train into the station at Sandy-on-Sea and spent a lovely lazy afternoon on the beach before he had to drive back home again.

Chuff-chuff, chuffitty -chuff, whoo . . . eee . . . eee . . .